# GRANNY'S FISH STORY

# GRANNY'S FISH STORY

written by PHYLLIS LA FARGE

pictures by GAHAN WILSON

Parents' Magazine Press / New York

*for the country granny*

Text copyright © 1975 by Phyllis La Farge
Illustrations copyright © 1975 by Gahan Wilson
All rights reserved
Printed in the United States of America

Library of Congress Cataloging in Publication Data
La Farge, Phyllis.
    Granny's fish story.
    SUMMARY: Julie introduces her friend Sarah to the
ways of the country during a visit to her grandmother's
house in the woods.
    [1. Grandparents—Fiction. 2. Country life—
Fiction] I. Wilson, Gahan, illus. II. Title.
PZ7.L139Gr  [E]  74-545
ISBN 0-8193-0760-2    ISBN 0-8193-0761-0 (lib. bdg.)

# Contents

## Granny's Invitation

The telephone rang. It was Julie's Granny, and she wanted to talk to Julie.

"How about coming to visit me?" Granny asked.

"When?" asked Julie.

"I'll pick you up tomorrow," said Granny, "for just overnight and the next day. Bring a friend if you like."

Bringing a friend would make a visit to Granny's even better than usual. Julie decided to invite Sarah. Granny lived in the country—and Julie knew Sarah had never been to the country before.

"What's your grandmother like?" asked Sarah the next day while they were waiting at Julie's house for Granny.

"She wears blue jeans and sneakers," said Julie, "and she lives in the woods. She knows lots about animals."

"She doesn't sound like other grandmothers," said Sarah.

"She isn't," said Julie.

She wondered if Sarah would like Granny . . . maybe she should have invited someone else. Sarah was wearing pants too fancy for the country. She didn't look ready for Granny's.

Then the doorbell rang. It was Granny. She hugged Julie and shook hands with Sarah.

"I'll drive up and bring you back tomorrow, girls," Mother said. "Have a good time."

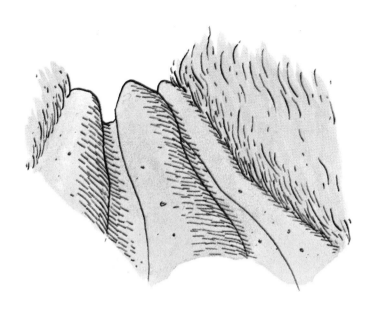

## Going to the Country

It took about an hour to get to Granny's. At last Granny turned off the paved road and drove down the dirt road that led to her house.

"Is this a real road?" asked Sarah. Julie thought Sarah sounded a little scared.

Granny laughed. "No, it isn't," she said. "I lived on a real road for years, with cars and buses going by, and then I decided I was going to live by a dirt road in the woods."

"What kind of animals live in the woods?" Sarah asked, looking out the car window into the trees.

"Oh, swamp halibut," said Granny, "and bush mackerel."

"I've never heard of them," said Sarah.

Now she really did sound scared.

"She's joking," said Julie. "There's no such thing as a swamp halibut or a bush mackerel."

But Julie didn't laugh out loud, because she remembered that only a few years before, she herself had believed in them.

"Look," said Granny. "Look at the grouse up ahead. It's taking a dust bath."

Granny drove very slowly. At last, when they were near enough to see clearly, the grouse got up, shook herself so that a little cloud of dust rose from her feathers, and walked into the bushes.

"She's pretty," said Sarah. "Will we see her again?"

"She's gone for now," Julie said.

## By the Pond

Suddenly they were at Granny's. Trev, Granny's puppy, barked from his doghouse. Down the hill from Granny's house was a pond.

"Can we go wading?" asked Sarah.

"Sure," said Granny.

"We can catch tadpoles, too," said Julie.

Sarah and Julie spent the afternoon by the pond.

They caught tadpoles and put them in jars which Granny had given them. They walked around the pond looking for the big frogs in the mud at the water's edge. Sometimes the frogs floated out into the pond with their legs spread and just their eyes above water.

Trev liked to hunt frogs, too. His tail wagged every time he was near one, but almost always the frog jumped out of reach just as he grabbed for it.

Julie caught four frogs and let them go again.

Sarah said she didn't want to touch a frog, but Julie said to her, "They don't feel bad," so she held one for a minute.

Granny brought juice and cookies down to the pond.

"Do you know," she said, pointing to the round disks on the head of the frog Julie was holding, "that those are the frog's ears?"

When they were tired of frogs, Julie and Sarah went wading again. Then they found a little water-fall and built a dam out of small stones. They were high in a tree beside the pond when Granny came to tell them it was nearly suppertime.

"Looks like a thunderstorm," Granny said, as they climbed down the tree.

Julie and Sarah had not noticed dark clouds billowing high in the sky.

## That Night

After supper, Granny played cards with Julie and Sarah. Then each girl drew her a picture and Granny read them a story. But the girls kept looking out the window at the lightning flickering in the dark sky.

"Are we really going to have a thunderstorm?" Sarah asked.

"Maybe it will pass us by," said Granny. She closed the book. "It's bedtime," she said.

Upstairs Granny tucked both girls in and kissed them goodnight. Then she turned off the lamp between their two beds.

When she was gone Sarah said to Julie, "I'm scared of thunderstorms—even in the city."

"So am I," said Julie.

They were both quiet for a minute or two. Then Sarah said, "What if swamp halibuts are real and—what was the other thing?"

"Bush mackerel," said Julie. "But they're not."

"But if they were real," said Sarah, "what do you think they'd look like?"

"Like fish, I think," said Julie, "but maybe furry, too, and with webbed feet."

"That's what I think," said Sarah.

Later Julie was awakened by Sarah's cries.

"Get them out of here! Help! Get them out of here!" she screamed.

Just then, a white flash of lightning lit the room, and thunder cracked so loudly that Julie thought it would split Granny's house.

"What's the matter?" Julie asked.

"The swamp halibut and bush mackerel are sitting on my bed! Get them off!"

"No, they're not," said Julie, "you're dreaming. I'll turn on the lamp."

But the lamp didn't work.

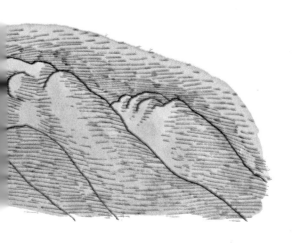

Now Julie was scared. She went out into the hall. "Granny!" she yelled, "Granny, where are you?"

A second later Granny appeared with a flashlight.

"Our lamp doesn't work," said Julie.

"Neither does mine," said Granny. "Sometimes the lights go out in a storm. A branch may fall on the line. What's wrong with Sarah?"

"She says a swamp halibut and a bush mackerel are sitting on her bed."

"I really should think before I speak," said Granny. "Not everyone knows enough to take what I say with a grain of salt—the way you do, Julie."

Together they went into Sarah and Julie's room.

"See, Sarah," said Granny, shining the beam of the flashlight into the corners of the room, "there are no swamp halibut and no bush mackerel here, and there never were."

"They were sitting on my bed," Sarah sobbed. "I saw them."

"You were dreaming," said Julie.

"No, I wasn't," said Sarah. "I hadn't even gone to sleep."

"You know what I think," said Granny. "I think we should all forget about sleeping while this storm is going on."

She led them down into the kitchen and lit the kerosene lamp she kept for times like this.

They sat together at the kitchen table.

## Granny's Story

"When I was your age," said Granny, "I used to be scared of thunderstorms. But one summer when I was visiting my grandmother there was a terrible thunderstorm just like this one.

"I cried and put my head under my pillow. But my grandmother made me get up. She made me sit on her lap by a window and look out at the storm and listen. It was beautiful and exciting. I remember hearing the first drops of rain the way you can hear them now. And after that, I was never scared again."

"Not even a little?" asked Julie.

"Maybe just a little," said Granny.

"Can we take turns sitting on your lap?" asked Sarah.

"If you'd like to," said Granny.

And so they did.

"It works," said Julie after a while, "I don't feel scared any more."

"Neither do I," said Sarah. "It's fun."

At last there was no more lightning, and the rumble of thunder was distant. The sound of rain lulled the girls.

"I'm sleepy," said Julie.

"Me, too," said Sarah.

After Granny had tucked them in again, Sarah asked her, "If swamp halibut and bush mackerel aren't real, who told you about them?"

"My grandmother," said Granny, "the same one who taught me not to be afraid of thunderstorms."

"Did you believe in them when she told you?" asked Sarah.

"Just a little," said Granny.

"That's all I believed in them," said Sarah, "just a little."

## The Next Day

By morning the sun was shining brightly—so brightly that for a moment Julie did not notice that the bedside lamp was shining brightly, too. Sarah was still asleep.

Julie turned off the lamp and ran downstairs. "Granny," she said, "the lights are back on."

"I know," said Granny. "The lines must have been repaired."

Granny and Julie had breakfast together.

"Granny," asked Julie, "even if you're not scared of thunderstorms and things, aren't you lonely sometimes here in the woods by yourself?"

"Lonely?" said Granny. "Sometimes I am, but it's the way I want to live. Besides, the trees and the pond are like friends."

"And you have Trev," said Julie.

"That's right," said Granny. "I have Trev."

Julie finished her cereal. Then she asked Granny another question. "When I'm big, do you think I'll be like you?"

"What do you mean?" asked Granny.

"Oh, you know, brave and good at country things."

"You already are," said Granny.

After Sarah had her breakfast, she and Julie played by the pond again. Sarah found a turtle that she wanted to take home along with her tadpoles. Julie found a green and yellow snake.

Granny said it was a garter snake and the turtle, a mud turtle.

After lunch Julie's mother came to drive them home.

"You were a good visitor, Sarah," said Granny. "Come again."

"I'd like to," Sarah said. "I wish I had a granny like you."

The girls sat in the back of the car on the way home. Very quietly Julie asked Sarah, "When you saw the swamp halibut and the bush mackerel—in your dream, I mean—did they really have feet?"

"Oh, yes," said Sarah. She thought carefully for a moment. "Only the bush mackerel had a furry body, but they both had little webbed feet."

*PHYLLIS LA FARGE* wrote *Granny's Fish Story* because the granny is "my daughter's grandmother—and my own mother." Furthermore, she admits, "I had worried about swamp halibuts for years."

A graduate of Radcliffe College and author of many children's books, Ms. La Farge now lives with her husband and two children in Hamden, Connecticut.

*GAHAN WILSON*, the nephew of a lion tamer, and a descendent of P.T. Barnum and William Jennings Bryan as well, is a professional cartoonist and illustrator of several children's books. His work has appeared in *Punch, Paris Match, National Lampoon*, and *Playboy*. Mr. Wilson lives with his wife, magazine writer Nancy Winters, and their two children in Boston.